LITTLE KNIGHT TO THE RESCUE

WRITTEN BY MICHÈLE DUFRESNE · ILLUSTRATED BY MAX STASUYK

Little Knight came out of his
hole and went outside.

He had on his helmet.
He had on his armor.
He had his sword.

"Help! Help! Help!"
cried a little voice.

Little Knight looked around.
Who was calling for help?

5

"I'm coming!"
shouted Little Knight.
"I'm coming to help you,
but where are you?"

"I'm in the forest!"
cried the little voice. "Help!"

"I'm coming!" shouted Little Knight. He ran into the forest.

"Where are you?" he shouted.

"Here I am," said the little voice. "I am by the tree."

Little Knight saw a girl mouse.
He saw vines around her tail.
"I am a knight," said Little Knight.
"I can help!"

"I will cut the vine
with my sword," said Little Knight.
Little Knight cut the vine.

"Thank you,"
said the girl mouse.
"Thank you for helping me.
Maybe I can help you someday."